THE WHOPPER

Rebecca Ashdown

templar publishing

Boris and Percy loved it when Grandma came to stay.
There was just one problem.
Grandma had been knitting again.

Boris quite liked his new jumper. Percy did NOT.
"Just right for walking the dog in!" cooed Grandma.

Walking the dog in his new jumper did make Percy feel **much** better.

Until it chased a cat . . .

. . . got tangled in brambles . . .

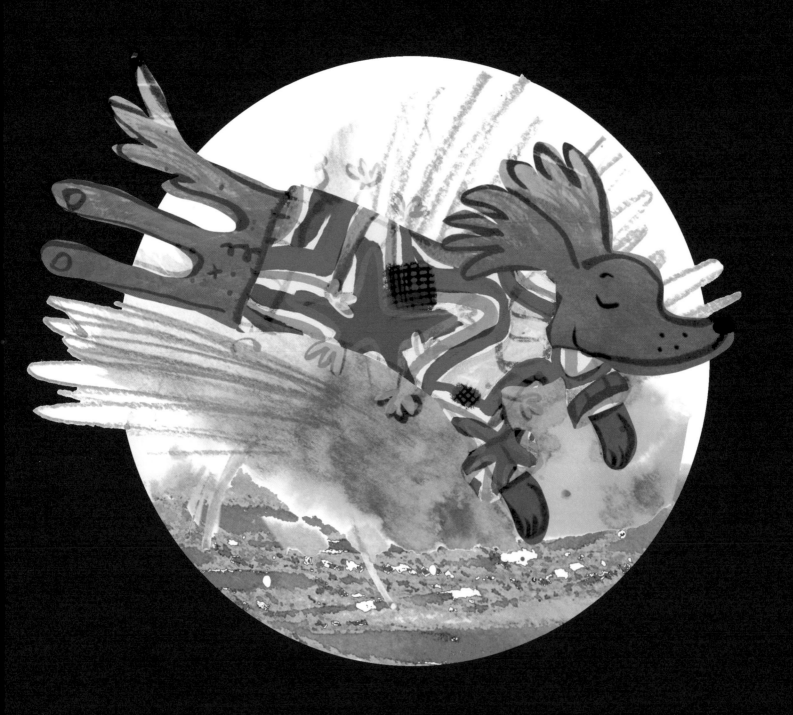

... splashed in a puddle . . .

. . . and rolled in something stinky.

There was only one place for the jumper now!

When they got home, it was clear something was missing.
"Percival! Where's your new jumper?" asked Mum.
"I've . . . er . . . lost it," he stammered.

Percy felt horrible.

He had told a whopping great lie.

Percy went to his room. He needed to be alone.

But then he noticed a strange creature.
"What are you?" gasped Percy.

"You told a big, hairy, monstrous lie," said the creature.
"It was a whopper. I am your Whopper!"

Percy showed the Whopper to his brother.
"What is THAT?" asked Boris.
"It's my lie, Boris. It's a Whopper," Percy whispered.
"And I don't know what to do with him."

The boys went downstairs. So did the Whopper.
That's when Percy discovered . . .

Grown-ups couldn't see the Whopper!

When Dad asked Percy when he'd last seen his jumper,
Percy said nothing. The Whopper began to **grow.**

When Mum said what a shame it was that he'd lost it,
Percy said nothing. The Whopper grew **bigger** still.

Even when Grandma left, Percy stayed silent.
By now, the Whopper was huge!

"It won't stop growing," said Percy.
"What am I going to do?"
"There's only one thing for it," said Boris.
"If that's your lie, you need to tell the truth."
"Never!" declared Percy.

That evening, the Whopper brushed his teeth, washed his hairy face and climbed into bed next to Percy.

It was a very **long** night indeed.
When the Whopper woke . . .

I'M HUNGRY!

he shouted.
And in **one** mouthful,
he **gobbled** the boy up.

Then, the Whopper got dressed,

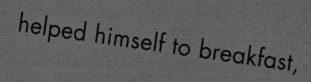

helped himself to breakfast,

played with the baby . . .

. . . and went to school.

It was a busy day for the Whopper.

When he got home, he was hungrier than ever.

And now he was looking at Boris...

Suddenly, the Whopper opened his mouth **wide**.

"Stop!" came a voice from the Whopper's belly.

"Mum!
I told a lie.
It was me!
I ruined Grandma's jumper!"

Then slowly, slowly, the Whopper began to fade away.

Until with a final **PLINK** . . . he was gone!

"Oh Percy!" said his mum. "Thank you for telling me the truth at last."

The next day, Percy decided to send his grandma a letter to say sorry for ruining the jumper.

A week later, a **parcel** arrived.

Percy **loved** getting parcels. There was just one problem . . .

. . . Grandma had been knitting AGAIN!

All my love —
Gran X

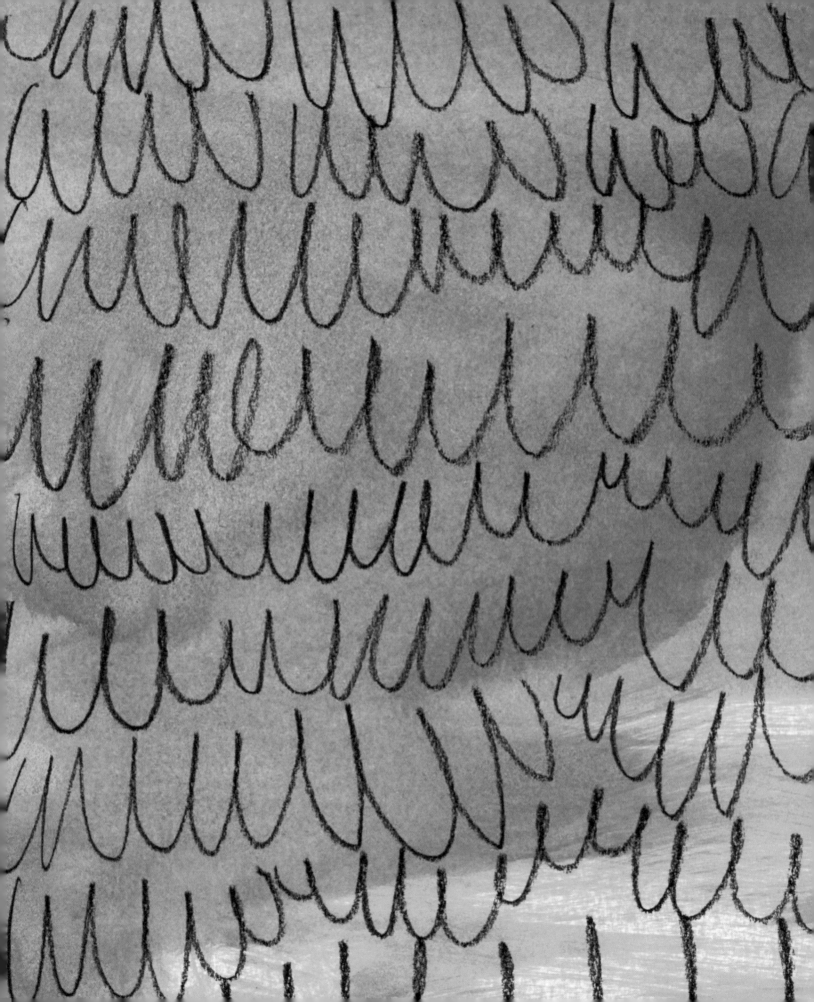